LEGO KNIGHTS' KINGDOM

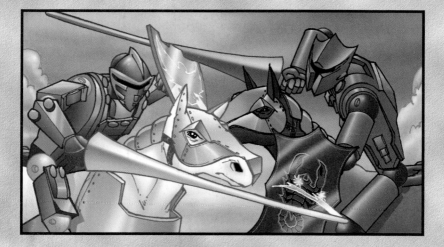

The Grand Tournament

by Daniel Lipkowitz

Illustrated by Mada Design Inc.

SCHOLASTIC INC.

New York   Toronto   London   Auckland   Sydney

Mexico City   New Delhi   Hong Kong   Buenos Aires

ISBN 0-439-70231-3

12 11 10 9 8 7 6 5 4   6 7 8 9/0

Designed by Rick DeMonico

Printed in the U.S.A.
First printing, April 2005

Chapter 1
A Dark Victory

ZZZAK! An electric bolt zig-zagged through the air, crashing into the shield of the black knight. The villagers of Morcia held their breath to see what would happen next.

The black knight laughed as the lightning splashed harmlessly off his shield. His horse galloped forward, raising a cloud of dust with its hooves. He lowered his long lance and took aim.

ZZZZAAKK! A huge bolt of lightning exploded from the lance. It crackled through the air and struck his opponent's shield. The other knight was thrown from his horse and onto the sandy floor of the Tournament Arena.

"Enough!" cried the fallen knight. "Your power is too great, Vladek. You win."

The Grand Tournament had begun.

Beneath his black helmet, Vladek grinned. It was going just as he had planned. One by one, the Knights of Morcia who had not yet become Shadow Knights would challenge him for the throne . . . and one by one, they would fall before his might.

Vladek was protected by dark and powerful magic. The lightning swords and lances of the other knights could never harm him. Soon he would be the champion and the next king of Morcia.

Vladek raised his lance. "The first of many victories!" he shouted triumphantly. "What knight will face me next? Who else wishes to be king of Morcia?"

Chapter 2
A Strange Warning

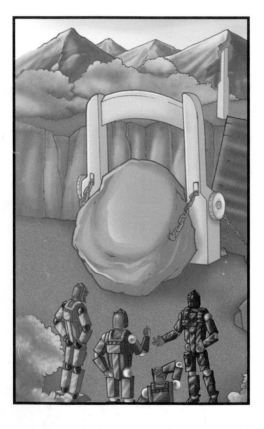

Four knights stood at the end of a path. They had travelled for many days, but they could go no further.

"What now?" asked Rascus, the green-armored knight. "We've reached our goal, but how do we get inside?"

On the other side of a deep chasm rose the tall tower of the Citadel of Orlan. The tower's stones were ancient and crumbling, and wrapped in ivy. A draw-bridge had once crossed the gap, but it had fallen in. Two moss-covered chains rose from the depths and looped around iron wheels on the stone archway at the end of the path. The ends of the chains were sunk deeply into a giant boulder that blocked the way.

"There's no way over, under, around, or through that stone," Danju, the purple-armored knight announced. "Someone put it here to block the way."

"Maybe Rascus could climb down the chains?" suggested Jayko, the blue-armored youngest knight. "He might be able to pull the drawbridge back up."

"I may be nimble," said Rascus, "but those chains are slippery. I'd fall right to the bottom of that gorge . . . if it even has one!"

Jayko turned to the red-armored knight. "What about you, Santis?" he asked. "You're the strongest knight in all of Morcia. Can you pick it up?"

"Sorry, Jayko," said Santis. "That rock's too big and heavy, even for me."

"No one can lift that stone," said a voice.

An old man stood on the path before them. He had

gray robes and a long white beard, and instead of a cane he leaned on a tall green spear.

"There is nothing for you here, knights," the old man said. "Forget this ancient ruin."

Jayko stepped forward. "We must enter the Citadel of Orlan!" he said. "The king of Morcia has sent us to find the Heart of the Shield!"

The old man shook his head. "You are brave," he said. "But the Citadel is a place of many dangers. Great challenges await those who seek to enter."

"Knights of Morcia fear no danger!" said Santis. "We will pass the challenges and find the Heart!"

"The mightiest have tried," the old man said, "but none has taken the Heart from the Guardian of the tower. The Citadel's magic makes him impossible to defeat."

"Then we will be the first," Jayko declared. "For we are the greatest knights in all of Morcia!" The young knight hoped that he was right. Becoming a hero was his dream, and saving the kingdom was certainly a hero's job.

The old man smiled sadly. "We shall see . . ."

His spear shone with a bright light, and the knights had to cover their eyes. When the light faded, the old man was gone.

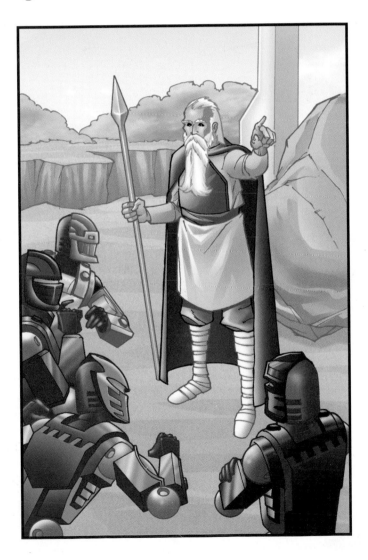

Chapter 3
A Place of Danger

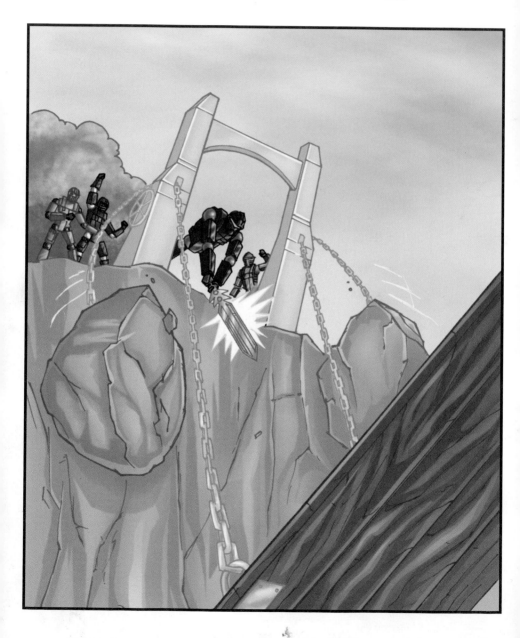

The knights searched, but the stranger was gone.

"What an odd old man," Rascus said.

"We'll prove him wrong and get the Heart," said Jayko. "I'm sure of it!"

"First we need to get to the Citadel," said Danju.

Santis nodded. Suddenly he raised his sword high above his head. "I may not be able to lift this rock . . ."

He brought the blade down with all of his strength. " . . . but I can still smash it!"

CRACK! The giant boulder split in two. The halves rolled off the cliff, plunging into the depths below.

There was a clinking and clanking. Pulled by the weight of the rocks, the chains wound around the wheels . . . and the drawbridge rose into place.

Danju laughed in surprise. "Well done, Knight of the Bear! An excellent plan!"

Santis coughed. From the look on his face, it was clear that he hadn't thought things that far through.

"Yeah," said the big knight. "That was my plan all along."

The knights crossed the drawbridge and entered the ancient castle. A few torches glowed and unseen creatures squeaked and skittered in the shadows.

"This place is even spookier than Vladek's castle," said Rascus with a shudder.

"We don't know what to expect here," said Danju. "Let's be careful."

"Take a look at this." Santis was standing near a large box on the floor. "What do you think is inside?"

"Maybe it's the Heart of the Shield," said Jayko. "Let's open it up!"

Danju was thoughtful. "Perhaps . . ." he said. He reached out with the tip of his sword and used it to raise the lid.

SHUNK! Danju pulled his sword out of the way just in time! A gigantic axe swung down from the ceiling, burying its blade in the stone floor in front of the chest.

". . . And then again, perhaps not," the Knight of the Wolf said.

Jayko gulped. "If one of us had been there . . ."

"Good thing we have Danju the Wise on our side!"
Rascus laughed. "That's two challenges down. Let's see
what's next!"

Chapter 4
A Foolish Mistake

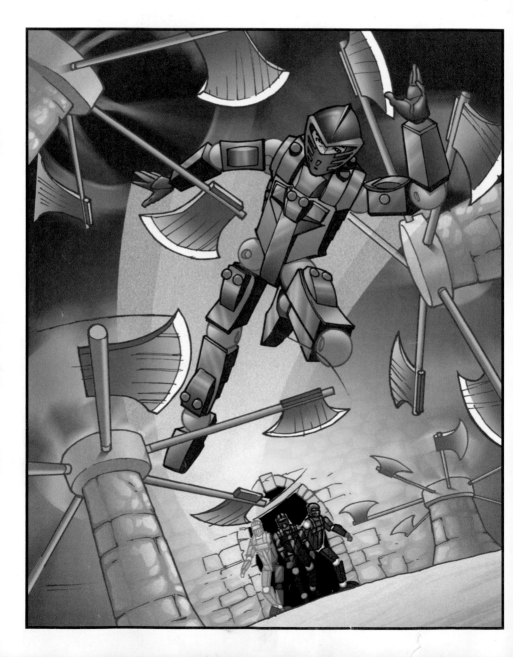

The knights had entered a long, narrow hallway with a smooth, sloping floor. It was filled with noise, and there was no mystery why: Everywhere they looked, deadly axes whirred and spun through the air.

Danju pointed past the whirling blades. "There's a lever in the wall. It might stop the axes."

"One of us will have to reach it first," said Santis.

Jayko knew that his moment had come. "Stand back," he said, "and leave this one to me!"

He took off running. As the first blade swung toward him, he leaped over it. He slid along the smooth stone floor as the second axe whirred over his head, then jumped to his feet and dashed past the next two.

In the blink of an eye, Jayko had safely reached the other side. He pulled the lever, and the axes slowed to a halt.

"Not bad, Jayko the Quick," said Santis. "Keep it up and you just might become that great hero you're always talking about."

Jayko grinned at the praise. "I can see the tower!" he called to the others as they made their way through the maze of frozen axes. "I'll meet you at its base!"

"Jayko, wait!" Danju shouted. He could see what lay ahead: a large, dark hole in the wall, and inside the hole, a pair of red lights that glittered like rubies.

But Jayko didn't hear him. What he did hear was a hiss like steam escaping from a giant kettle. A monstrous serpent lunged out of the darkness, its long white fangs snapping the air where Jayko had stood a moment before!

"I've got him!" said Santis, holding the blue knight just out of reach of the serpent's teeth. "Young fool, you were nearly that thing's supper!"

Rascus jumped onto the snake's head and lashed a rope around its jaws. It bucked like a wild horse, until the green knight finally sealed it back in its cave.

Danju was not at all pleased with Jayko's carelessness. "King Mathias is depending on us to save Morcia

from Vladek," he told the young knight. "You must learn to think before you act. Don't just charge ahead. Choose your moment!"

"I'm sorry." Jayko lowered his head. "I'll do better next time."

Danju looked at him. "You know, Jayko, I think you will," he said, thoughtfully. "You may just surprise us all."

Chapter 5
A Final Challenge

Finally the knights reached the base of the ivy-covered tower.

"But there's no door!" said Santis.

"And yet we must get inside," said Danju.

"I could smash down the wall," Santis suggested, but Rascus shook his head and pointed up.

"The answer, my friends," he said, "lies above you!"

As the other knights watched, Rascus took a running start and leaped onto the side of the tower. He grabbed hold of a vine and began to climb. Soon he had scrambled almost halfway to the top.

"There's a lever up here," he called down to the others. "Let's see what happens when I pull it!"

A hidden door swung open, revealing a narrow spiral staircase. Rascus jumped down, and together the four knights began the long climb to the top.

After what felt like hours, they approached the top of the stairs. The knights could feel that they were nearing the end of their long quest.

"We've done it!" said Jayko. "We've passed all of the Citadel's challenges! The Heart of the Shield is ours!"

"Not yet," a voice boomed.

At the top of the tower was a room full of light. A tall figure in white and gold armor stood in the center of the room. He held a golden sword, and in the center of his shield was a circular stone. It was the Heart of the Shield, the prize that the knights had come to find.

"You have done well, Knights of Morcia," said the Guardian of the Citadel. "But one more test awaits you."

Jayko drew his own sword and stepped forward. "So it's a fight that you want?" he asked. "Then we'll be happy to —"

Danju put his hand on Jayko's shoulder. "Wait, Jayko," he said. "We were told that the Guardian could not be defeated in

battle. Let us try another way."

He set down his sword and shield and kneeled before the Guardian.

"Noble knight, the Heart of the Shield of Ages is needed to defeat a great evil," he said. "Lord Vladek has used dark magic to take over Morcia. Only the Heart can stand against him. May we please take it to save our kingdom?"

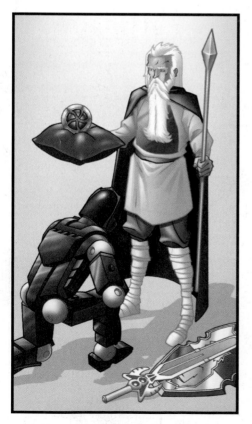

The Guardian's golden armor shimmered and vanished. In his place stood the mysterious old man from the path. "You have passed the final test, wise Knight of Morcia," he said with a smile. "The Heart of the Shield is yours!"

Chapter 6
A Hero Rises

The Grand Tournament was nearly over.

"Are there no more challengers?" Vladek called out. "Then it seems Morcia has a new king!"

"Not so fast!" A whisper, then a roar ran through the audience.

Vladek stared. "Mathias?!"

It *was* King Mathias.

Vladek recovered quickly. "An impostor," he said with a sneer. "King Mathias is gone. But even if he were here, he, too, would fall before my power."

"I will not be your challenger today, Vladek," said Mathias. He waved his arm toward the gate.

A knight rode into the arena with the sun at his back. He held his lance and shield at the ready. Vladek squinted to make out the symbol on his shield.

"Is that old Danju the Wolf?" he said. "Or mighty Santis the Bear? Or is it Rascus the Monkey?"

"Not today," the knight replied. His blue armor gleamed in the light. "You'll have to make do with Jayko the Hawk."

"A mere boy?" Vladek asked. "This will be even easier than I expected! But first . . . Shadow Knights, seize that false king!"

"No one shall harm the king!" Danju, Santis, and Rascus stood beside Mathias. Knights and king together drew their swords.

Vladek chuckled. "They'll be no match for my Shadow Knights," he said. "In the meantime, young Hawkling, let us joust!"

Jayko turned to face Vladek. Everything depended on this battle. If Vladek was not defeated, nothing would stop him from becoming Morcia's king. Jayko couldn't let that happen!

The two knights took their places at opposite ends of the arena. They lowered their lances and raised their shields.

Jayko's horse charged forward. "For King, for Morcia, for the Code!" he shouted as he fired a blast of lightning from his lance.

The bolt struck Vladek's shield, but the black knight

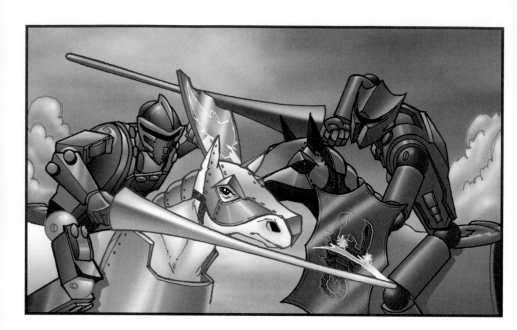

simply laughed and fired his own lightning in return. Powered by dark magic, Vladek's blast struck Jayko's shield with incredible force.

Jayko was tossed right out of his saddle. Dropping his lance as he fell, he landed on his shield and rolled to his feet. He drew his sword and pointed it at Vladek.

"Still some fight in you?" Vladek asked. "Good!" He leaped from his horse and drew his own blade.

Jayko flung a bolt of lightning from his sword. His aim was perfect, but Vladek barely noticed it splash off his shield.

"What made you think you could challenge me, little Hawkling?" he asked mockingly. "Were you hoping to be a hero?" The dark knight gave a cruel laugh. "Fool! My magic protects me." He hurled another blast at Jayko. The young knight staggered back, barely raising his shield in time. His sword fell from his numbed fingers.

There was only one chance! Jayko reached for the pouch at his belt. The black knight's eyes narrowed when he saw the object in Jayko's hand.

"So, you and your friends found the Heart of the Shield," Vladek hissed. "Perhaps its power can give you a fighting chance."

A blast of lightning knocked the Heart from Jayko's hands.

". . . But I doubt it."

Vladek aimed his sword straight at Jayko.

"Now and forever, Morcia will be *mine*!" he proclaimed in triumph.

"*Never!*" shouted Jayko. Knowing that he couldn't

dodge Vladek's lightning, he hurled himself toward the Heart of the Shield. His fingers closed around the magic stone, then he stood and turned to face Vladek.

Now the Heart glowed brightly in the center of Jayko's shield. Vladek's mightiest blast struck it . . . and was returned with ten times the power!

Vladek was thrown through the air. Engulfed in lightning, he dropped his sword and shield as he crumpled to the ground, defeated.

"Enough . . ." Vladek whispered hoarsely. "You win, Jayko the Hawk."

The silence was broken by thunderous applause. Everyone began cheering the brave young knight. The other knights surrounded Jayko. "You did it, Jayko!" said Danju. "When Vladek's magic was defeated, his spell over the Shadow Knights was broken. The king is safe, and Morcia is free!"

"My brave knights," said Mathias, "everyone in Morcia owes you their freedom."

He turned to Jayko. "And we owe particular thanks to you, Jayko. You have won the Grand Tournament. By rights, you are Morcia's new king."

Jayko grinned. "Thank you, Your Majesty, but I don't think I'm quite ready for that yet," he said. "I'd rather be a great hero first."

"After today, no one will doubt that you are exactly that," said Mathias with a kind smile. He turned to face the arena audience. "It appears I shall be king a little longer," he told the cheering crowd. "And it seems that Morcia has four new heroes!"

"Hooray for the heroes!" came the cry from all the knights and villagers of Morcia. "Hooray for Jayko! Hooray for Danju! Hooray for Santis! Hooray for Rascus! Hip hip hooray!"

The knights' quest was at an end. But in Morcia, the next adventure is always just around the corner!

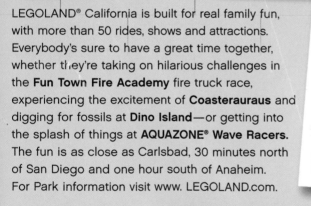